To Alana Angel, who loves the water.
Wishing you a life full of treasures.

First American Edition 2017
Kane Miller, A Division of EDC Publishing

Text and illustration copyright © 2017 by Henning Löhlein
Design copyright © 2017 by The Templar Company Limited

First published in the UK in 2017 by Templar Publishing,
part of the Bonnier Publishing Group

For information contact:
Kane Miller, A Division of EDC Publishing
PO Box 470663
Tulsa, OK 74147-0663
www.kanemiller.com
www.edcpub.com
www.usbornebooksandmore.com

Library of Congress Control Number: 2017941138

Printed in China
1 2 3 4 5 6 7 8 9 10

ISBN: 978-1-61067-708-0

LUDWIG THE SEA DOG

Henning Löhlein

Kane Miller
A DIVISION OF EDC PUBLISHING

Ludwig was very excited – he'd always wanted to visit the sea.
Of course he'd help Peter. There was just one problem . . .

Ludwig lived in a world of books. The closest he'd ever been to water was when he and his friends played on a picture of a pond.

Ludwig had read a lot about life underwater. In his dreams, the ocean was full of strange creatures and wonderful adventures.

There was one book
about the deep blue sea
that looked particularly exciting,
but his friends would not let him open it.

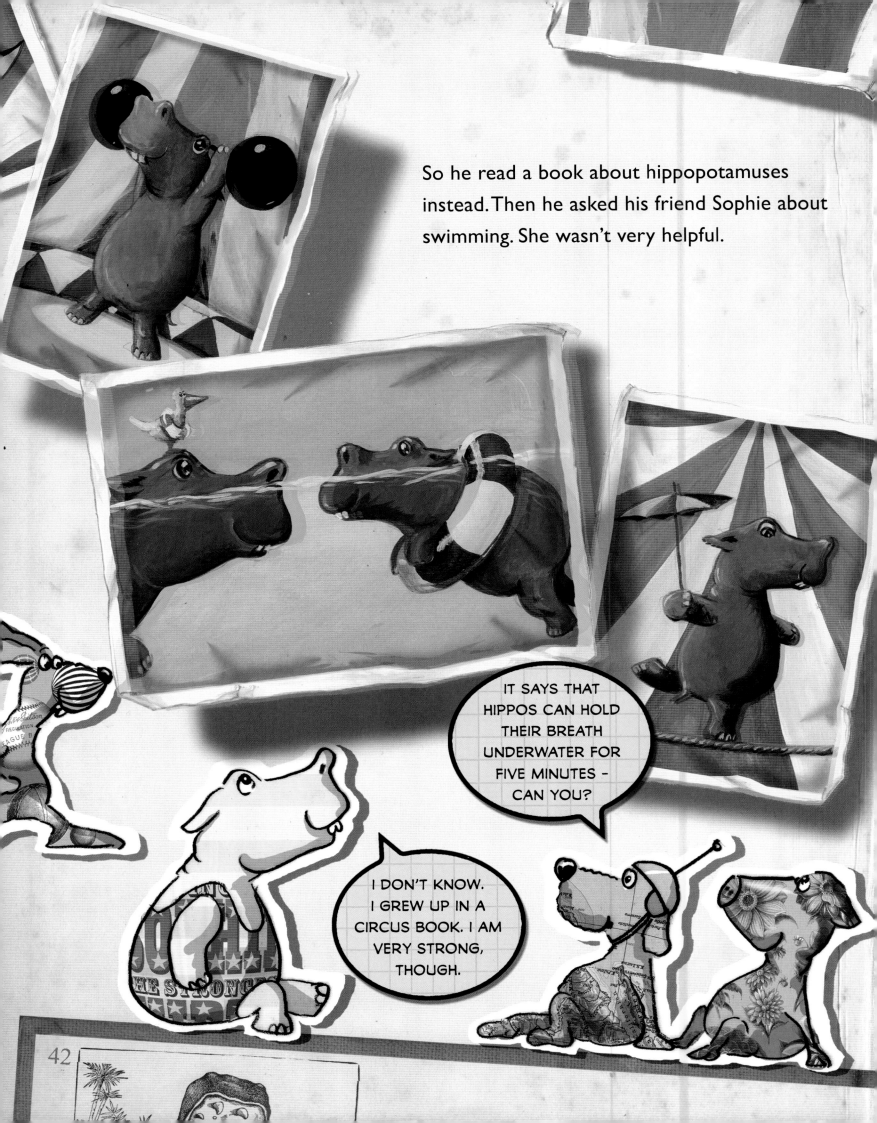

So he read a book about hippopotamuses instead. Then he asked his friend Sophie about swimming. She wasn't very helpful.

Ludwig decided there was only one thing for it.

He put on his swimming trunks,

he found some goggles,

and he got ready to dive into . . .

Things didn't go very well, and Ludwig's friends had to help him out.

This time, Ludwig didn't hesitate. He went straight to the book about the deep blue sea and pulled open the cover.
The creatures inside thrashed about, and his friends ran away.

Sophie didn't look where she was going.

His friends pulled him out and shook the water off him.

HOW CAN I HELP PETER WHEN I CAN'T EVEN GET WET?

Then they put him in a nearby book so he dried flat.

The fairy queen waved her wand.

Then she tamed the sea creatures, turned the pages of the book into real water and gave Ludwig a magic spell so he could swim.

Ludwig swam deeper and deeper. He passed sausage fish and all sorts of colorful creatures. It was more wonderful than he had ever imagined.

Ludwig dived into a magical world.

The submarine wasn't in good shape,
but Ludwig knew how to fix it. There was just
one problem — he couldn't get to the engine.

And then he saw something he wasn't expecting.

Swimming through the water towards him were all his friends.

Together, they lifted up the submarine so Ludwig could fix the engine.
Then they all swam to the surface . . .

Ludwig wondered where his next adventure would take him.